THE SNOW DANCER

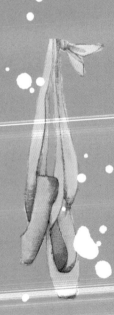

by Addie Boswell   illustrated by Mercè López

two lions

Published by Two Lions, New York
www.apub.com

Amazon, the Amazon logo, and Two Lions are trademarks of Amazon.com, Inc., or its affiliates.
ISBN-13: 9781542093170 (hardcover) • ISBN-10: 1542093171 (hardcover)

The illustrations are rendered in acrylic, graphite, and digital media.

Book design by Abby Dening • Printed in China

First Edition
10 9 8 7 6 5 4 3 2 1

For Tokey, and our snow adventures

—A. B.

To the four dancers who have helped me during this trip:
Irene, Kayoko, Ximel, and my dear "Funk attempt"

—M. L.

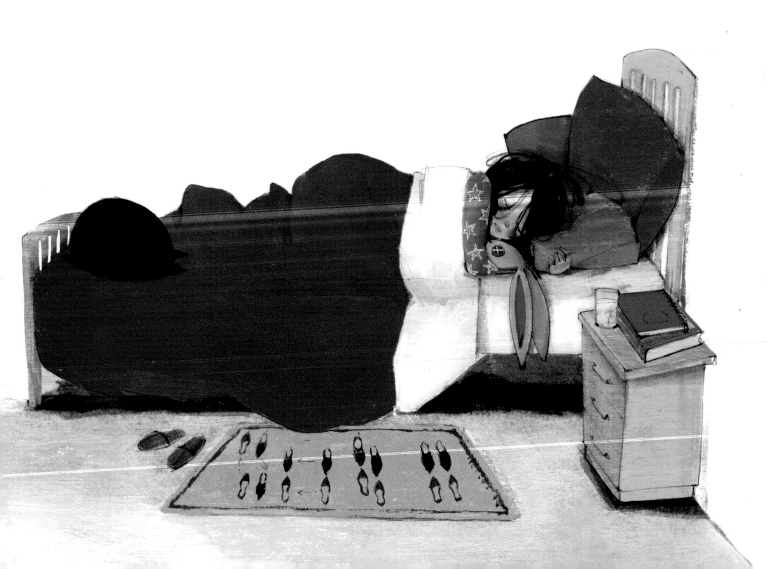

Sofia was asleep when the snowflakes came.

All through the night they fell—
   frosting the rooftops, fluffing the sidewalks,
      laying fuzzy hats on the fire hydrants.

When she woke, Sofia flew to the window.

"Snow day?" she asked.

"Snow day," she said.

"SNOW DAY!" she cheered.

Her voice hung in the still air.
No buses squealed.
No cars honked.
No neighbors shouted.

Her city—and all its sounds—had disappeared.

Sofia bundled out of the sleeping house.
She sniffed the cold, clean air and tasted the sparkling snow.

WHOOOMPH!

She fell down the hidden steps.

CRINCH.

CRUNCH.

CRINCH.

CRUNCH.

She hopscotched down the invisible sidewalk.

SLISH, SLUSSSSSSSSSSH.

SLISH, SLUSSSSSSSSSSH.

She skated across the frozen street.

She slid to a stop
at the top of the park.

The sun shone like a giant spotlight.
The soccer field gleamed
like a giant stage.

There wasn't a single set of footprints.

Yet.

Sofia leaped.

She twirled.

She made patterns with her footprints.

CRINCH. CRUNCH. CRINCH. CRUNCH.

She drew lines with her shuffles.

SLISH, SLUSSSSSSSSSSSH. SLISH, SLUSSSSSSSSSSSSH.

She danced a whole ballet into the silence.

Until . . .

. . . children appeared at the top of the hill.

"Look!" whispered a little girl. "A snow fairy!"

But the other kids didn't hear.
They saw the giant spotlight
and the giant stage.

They shouted, "SNOW DAY!"
as they ran skelter-melter down the hill.

"STOP!" Sofia said.

"WAIT!"

"LISTEN!"

But the kids didn't stop.
They were too busy running and jumping,
laughing and yelling, pushing and falling.

Scattering all of Sofia's beautiful silence.

A little girl tugged on her scarf.
"Are you a Snow Fairy?"

"I'm not a fairy. I'm just a dancer,"
sniffled Sofia.

"What does a Snow Dancer do?"

Sofia thought for a moment.
She stood up a little straighter.

"A Snow Dancer can do ANYTHING."

She reached out her hand.
"I'll show you."

The other kids stomped roads that crisscrossed the stage.
CRONCH. CRONCH. CRONCH. CRONCH.

And Sofia and her new friend
twirled through the blank spaces.

The other kids cannonballed themselves into the snowdrifts.

KA-SPLOOSH!   KA-SPLOOSH!

And Sofia and her new friend leaped
over them on their tiptoes.

They skated and swirled and slid until . . .

a snowball landed

SPLAT!

right on Sofia's shoulder.

The kids froze.
A silence fell over the park.

The Snow Dancer looked to her sidekick.
They shared a secret smile.
A secret SNOW DANCER smile.

"SNOWBALL FIGHT!" Sofia shouted.

Soon the kids were too tired to throw one more snowball.
They lay scattered in the snow
and listened to the sounds moving closer.

Snowplows pulled out.

SCREEEEEEETCH.
SCREEEEEEEEEETCH.
SCRAAAPE.

Buses started their engines.
HUFF, HUFF,
HARROOM.

And parents called
their kids home
to shovel.

Sofia spread her arms and gave
her new friend a grand curtsy.

The girl curtsied back.

Then the Snow Dancer twirled in the white world once more
and turned for home, dancing in her frozen footprints.

CRINCH.   CRUNCH.   CRINCH.

CRUNCH.

SLISH, SLUSSSSSSSSSH.   SLISH, SLUSSSSSSSSSH.

WHOOOMPH!

At home, Sofia snuggled up with a mug of cocoa.

SNIFFLE, SNIFFLE, SSSIIIIIIIGH.

Outside, the world sparkled and glistened.
"Snow day," Sofia whispered.